To my one true love and our three magical babies who make my life oh so sweet. Thank you for always believing I can fly.

This spooky-sweet tale is all about
a little witch named Andi.
She looks polite, but beware,
she may swipe your candy.

Those Halloween treats,
you've carefully sorted?
She'll conjure a charm to snatch
up what you've hoarded.

She comes late at night,
    so you'll never catch her,
But you'll know she's the culprit,
    by reading her letter.

She'll probably write that
    candy's not worth it,
It's bad for your teeth,
    and teeth don't deserve it.

And it's not just your mouth
   but your chest and your belly.
She might even add that it
   makes your feet smelly!

But don't fret, not yet,
   this candy thief's considerate.
She'll leave a few behind for you,
   including your most favorite.

So who is this Andi,
 you rightly want to know?
Our story starts in Boo-ville,
 many years ago.

When she was small, four-feet tall,
 having just turned eight,
And living with her parents
 and cat Snowball the Great.

She had red curly locks,
     freckled cheeks and chin,
And bright blue eyes framed
     by sun-kissed skin.

That might sound nice,
     by most reports,
But Boo-ville witches
     favored green warts.

Her long days at witch school
 didn't exactly go well.
 The Witch Academy often made her
 want to crawl into a shell.

It didn't help that Andi
 couldn't cast a spell.
 Nor could she look scary, which
 made her troll teacher yell.

Her classmates weren't nice.
"You're no witch," they would chant,
"You look funny and sound weird,
 you couldn't conjure up an ant!"

Sometimes their teasing
 made her feel blue.
But that didn't stop Andi,
 because of a secret she knew.

She could twirl, jump and speed
  higher and faster than all,
In fact Andi flew so well,
  she took not a single fall.

Ms. Bones gave her the star charm,
  she was so impressed.
Andi's classmates, however,
  were simply furious.

The truth was they were jealous,
which also made them sour.
It bothered them to see her win
at such a challenging power.

So they doubled down on teasing,
even taunting Andi's cat.
They also broke her broomstick
and laughingly slimed her hat.

This blow was one too many
to simply shake it off.
So Andi cried that night to mom,
who made slug stroganoff.

But even her favorite dinner
could not solve this mess.
Andi wanted them to pay,
for them to feel distress.

That night she plotted her revenge,
a darkly clever scheme.
She'd wreck what THEY loved best,
She'd cancel Halloween!

A few days later, when it was time,
she skipped the Halloween traditions.
Instead she rode her broom up high
so as not to raise suspicions.

Later as the people slept,
　　she swept into each house,
Swiping all the humans' treats,
　　soundless as a mouse.

　　She wasn't sure that it was right
　　　　to steal the others' fun.
　　But she ignored that icky feeling,
　　　　until her job was all done.

The next day at school was strange.
　　The witch bullies all seemed sad.
They teased her just the same of course,
　　but they didn't seem so glad.

They didn't know, or didn't guess,
　　that it was their cruel taunting
That inspired Andi's first – not last –
　　mischievous candy jaunting.

Indeed, she carried out her scheme
throughout the years in secret.
She was on a roll, way out of control,
nabbing candy just to keep it.

It went on like that for years and years,
candy here, then poof, it's gone.
So people just stopped buying it,
   which made the factories all shut down.

No more factories meant no more candy,
   and that meant no more reason,
For any child to trick or treat,
   or celebrate the season.
It seemed Halloween was done-for,
   until Andi bravely spoke.
"I can help," she said
   and it was true—she sure had hoped.

"I have candy, loads of it,
    that I can soon distribute!
But only if you stop your taunts
    and take a kinder route!"
Then she conjured the candy she'd stolen
    into her magical bag.
The crowd was silent for a moment
    then "yes!" cried a popular hag.

"We can and shall be better,
each of us must try.
Apparently our differences
can sometimes help us fly."

The others quite agreed with this,
"Let's stop this teasing war!

If we're going to save the day tonight,
then kindness must be restored!"

Then they fretted 'cause too much sugar
 isn't good for you
So the mindful witches measured out
 a healthier amount to chew.

They figured dentists and doctors
 would agree that it's okay
  To enjoy a "just-right" number
   of fun treats the next day.

Boo-ville filled with cheers and glee,
  as the witches all decreed,
"We've got a plan that's sure to work,
  Go Andi, take the lead!"

So Andi and her faithful cat
  hopped on her fabulous broomstick,
And flew off to deliver the treats
  before the first chants of "Trick...".

The rest of the witches clapped and shouted,
   "You can do it, Andi!
We believe in you and trust,
   you'll save the day with candy!"

And deliver it, she did!
   It was a magical wonder!
Right-sized piles of favorite treats
   left as children slumbered.

Back in Boo-ville, happy witches
danced across the skies,
This time casting happy spells,
not mean ones that cause surprise.
They held a broom parade
all in Andi's honor,
Celebrating that Halloween
would not be a total goner.

Since then Andi always leaves
    each child their fave few sweets.
But when a Halloween bag spills over,
    she snags the extra treats.

And it's not so she can eat them,
    oh my goodness no,
To help your tummy and your teeth,
    she'll take a few to-go.

These she'll save as extra treats
to give out down the road,
And brighten the day of other kids
who couldn't get a load.

for Andi!

for me!

So always sort your treats
before you go to bed.
She'll leave your faves, and put the rest
in her giveaway shed.

When you wake, you'll find her note,
explaining why she bothers,
"To save your tummy bloat," she'll say,
"And also help out others."
So go ahead, enjoy those sweets,
and take her wise advice -
The best treats taste even better,
when you're kind and acting nice.

the end

Made in the USA
Coppell, TX
08 October 2021